Dan Urquhart

The Sraddha

Dan Urquhart

The Sraddha

Reprint of the original, first published in 1857.

1st Edition 2023 | ISBN: 978-3-37516-082-1

Salzwasser Verlag is an imprint of Outlook Verlagsgesellschaft mbH.

Verlag (Publisher): Outlook Verlag GmbH, Zeilweg 44, 60439 Frankfurt, Deutschland
Vertretungsberechtigt (Authorized to represent): E. Roepke, Zeilweg 44, 60439 Frankfurt, Deutschland
Druck (Print): Books on Demand GmbH, In de Tarpen 42, 22848 Norderstedt, Deutschland

THE SRADDHA,

THE KEYSTONE OF THE

BRAHMINICAL, BUDDHISTIC, AND ARIAN RELIGIONS,

AS ILLUSTRATIVE OF

THE DOGMA AND DUTY OF ADOPTION

AMONG THE

PRINCES AND PEOPLE OF INDIA.

By D. URQUHART

London:

PUBLISHED BY DAVID BRYCE,

AMEN CORNER, PATERNOSTER ROW.

1857.

THIS fragment of a Work now in the Press, but of which
the publication may be delayed, is printed off with the view
of calling attention to the violation of usage and religion uncon-
sciously practised by the British rulers of India, and which,
unless arrested, must at no distant period bring the dismember-
ment of the British Empire.

London, May 30th, 1857.

THE SRADDHA.

ANCESTRAL WORSHIP AND LAW OF ADOPTION.

THIS ceremony belongs to no one race or creed, for it is the link between the races, and the common matrix of their creeds; it transcends all other branches in importance, and exceeds them in difficulty. It cannot be dealt with as history, or as metaphysics, for both are born from it: in the mysteries of life and love its spring is hidden, and is not to be found unless sought for there. As on entering a sacred grove, here also we must deposit the profane vestment of opinion, nor would this (if practicable) be all; we must surrender for a time our judgment as well, and give up our wisdom as our folly; for a clear eye will not give you to know man as if he were a crystal or a plant: the eye to see him by is the soul. Seek to know as a child seeks to know, and you will be able to judge as a man ought to judge; for this, speculativeness must give place to reverence, knowledge to ignorance, science to superstition.

That this appeal is not misplaced, nor the awe with which I approach the subject groundless, appears in this: that no writer in any age or country has handled it. Connected as it is, no less with the actual government of India than with the interpretation of the monuments of Egypt—interwoven as it is with the institutes and laws of all the great states of antiquity, and followed by one half of the present human family—this neglect is only to be attributed to an incompatibility of assimilation between its nature and our ideas. A splendid task remains yet to be undertaken; when accomplished, the world of letters and of laws will learn that it itself had once an ancestry of heart. I presume not to handle such weighty matters, but yet from the field may pluck some ears of grain for present use.

The duty of the primitive child to the parent extended to every service that could be rendered, to every sacrifice that could be made. The most menial offices had to be fulfilled, and life itself had to be surrendered, if necessary, for the parent's well-being, or, as we see in the cases of Abraham and of Jephtha, at his desire.

This relationship did not close with life : it was the part of the son to "serve his parents dead as he had served them living ;" a service accomplished through their notion of death, which enabled him still to perform equally his twofold duty of doing reverence and providing food.

A touching scene is related by some African traveller of an Abyssinian woman placing a morsel of bread in the mouth of her dead child : the most artless expression of grief and desire, in presence of the mystery of death, while startling and new. The spirit had fled, naked and helpless, into cold space ; it was not dead—it could not die ; reasoning was not wanted ; it returned nightly in visions and in dreams. Like despotism, materialism is modern ; like liberty, spiritualism is ancient ; not that of the metaphysician, but of the child. The ghost must want sustenance, it must require clothing ; who but its kin on earth could furnish it ? but by what way could it be reached ? where was the messenger ?

This sense is universal ; the methods employed, dissimilar. In the grosser mythologies, death itself was used as a vehicle, and animals, attendants, or wives were entombed with the corpse, or poisoned, or left to perish by hunger ; but here another process was employed.

A reversed flame has always been the symbol of death ; but the production of flame is not less a mystery than death itself. It suggests even to us the imagery for life, for soul, for faith, for genius. Light springing from darkness—flame flowing out of cold matter, incessantly flying from earth to heaven, ascending, as it were, to its native sky, and seeming to carry up with it the substance upon which it feeds :—of the nature of the stars, assigned as the abode to the departed, to whose flight, as to that of the ancestors, the pathless air was no obstacle ; this was the vehicle. To flame, then, offerings were consigned as the messenger of the gods.

The Rig Veda opens with this passage, which, as containing

the elementary part of faith, is recited before reading the Sacred Books :

" I praise divine fire, primevally consecrated, the efficient performer of a solemn ceremony, the chief agent of a sacrifice."

The Hindus have a ritual which may have been, like our own, subjected to interpolation, but of which the framework is older than any writings or institutes. There we find fire personified thus:

" Fire, approach to taste (my offering), thou, who art praised for the *gift of oblations*. Sit down on this grass, thou, who art the *complete performer* of the solemn sacrifice." *

Why it is praised and invoked, this passage shows :

" Accept these offerings ; carry them to the ancestors ; THOU KNOWEST THY OFFICE," or " thy WAY."

It was not ordinary fire that was employed, but a flame obtained in that manner which philosophers have imagined to have first conferred on man the knowledge and possession of this wonderful element—the friction of the branches of trees. This is the " *Primevally* consecrated fire." Such are the words of the Vedas. What is implied in " Primevally," save that the process was used by all before their dispersion or their schisms? and so we find it amongst Buddhists or Brahmins, Arians or Chinese, Romans or Mexicans. Humboldt, describing the process employed by the latter people to relight the sacred fire, when at the close of every 52nd year they had extinguished it, employs the very terms of the Puranas in prescribing to the Hindus the form of the same ceremony. A block of wood, five inches cube hollowed into a cup, is drilled with a spindle of itself till it flames ; a consecrated tree is used for this purpose—the *Sami* or Soma (moon-plant), thence entitled *Arani*, or "mother of fire." † Here was surely no idea of fire as an element, but solely as a sacrificer ; and, whether as to the primitiveness of the process, or object, or universality and uniformity of the practice, it is impossible to ascend higher ; here we have reached the fountain head, not of this rite, but of ritual.

The Romans had but one fire for the whole state continually

* *As. Res.*, v. vii., pp. 272, 3.

† If by any accident the dire calamity of the extinction of the sacred fire befell the Romans, it was reproduced by the Pontifex Maximus from two pieces of the *Arbor Felix.*—*Festus v. Ignis.*

burning, and whence sacrificial flame was distributed; but the Brahmin or Alhan, and indeed all the "twice born" who keep "consecrated hearths," had the sacred fire produced for each. It was made on his investment with the sacrificial cord, it supplied the fire for all sacred offices during life, lit his funeral pyre, with which it became extinct.

As actually practised, the Sraddha has in the first instance to restore to the spirit the organs destroyed by cremation. The ceremonies used for this end occupy the period of mourning; the spirit has then to be elevated to the sphere,* and placed in the rank of the former ancestors. This operation is not concluded till the end of a year; and in and by the performance of multiplied solemn acts, but always consisting in the offering of sustenance.

But it did not suffice to commit the offering to the flame; the assurance was required that they had received it; besides, the ancestors were to be no less honoured than fed; they required a banqueting hall, no less than a banquet. There was then no temple, no grave or tomb; a place had still to be fixed upon, and to it they had to be *brought down.* In this, great dexterity and profound science were required; for the ancestors, needy and dependent, were also haughty and punctilious. If the scenes, circumstances, thoughts, words, motions of the sacrificers and attendants were satisfactory and pleasing, then, on being invited by "race and name," they came and took their places according to their rank, on small cushions made of folded blades of grass.

It was a scene of grave, solemn, and affectionate family meeting; not one of grief and tumult. "Unwillingly do the manes taste the tears and rheum shed by their kinsmen; then do not wail, but diligently perform the obsequies of the dead!" "By the Hindu ritual," says Macpherson, "six ancestors only were called upon by name,† but, amongst the hill tribes, all the ancestors are

---

* "Fire thou wert lighted by him—may he therefore be reproduced from thee that he may attain the region of celestial bliss. May this offering be auspicious!"—*As. Res.,* v. vii., p. 242.

† "The food is offered to six ancestors by name, with the usual preparatory vow and prayers, and with the formality of placing three blades of grass as a seat for each ancestor."—*As. Res.,* v. vii., p. 270.

The Romans, in like manner, enumerated to the sixth degree; that is to say, to the Tritavus by name.

called upon. The worship of deceased ancestors is a striking and important feature of the Khond religion. The more distinguished fathers of the tribe, of its branches, or of its subdivisions, are all remembered by the priests, their sanctity growing with the remoteness of the period of their deaths; and they are invoked in endless array after the gods. * * * They are propitiated upon every occasion of public worship whatever; and it is said that a perfectly accomplished priest takes between three and four hours to recite his roll of beads."

The Institutes of Menu and the Vedas limit the "calling by name" to the three ancestors. These gradations mark the relative antiquity of the Vedas, the ritual, and the practices of the hill tribes.

The knowledge of these names thus became a mystery, affording to the Sacerdotal class material for the establishment of power and influence. Here is the explanation of the calling on the *names* of gods, &c.; of the potency attributed in the Greek mysteries to the utterance of certain names, some of which could stop the moon in her course, some the sun, some disturb the order of nature, and shake the universe. These names were not Greek, but Barbarian; and the knowledge of them constituted the mystery.

Now for the scene of this festival. We stand in an age when nothing of what is ancient had as yet existence; when nothing stood consecrated by time; when the tide of tradition had not yet commenced to roll; when each process, if new, had reference to its purpose, and had its key either in extant ideas or prevailing circumstances; how, then, consecrate a spot, when all earth was alike? how choose a direction? Yet they did consecrate a spot, and it was by drawing geometrical lines, derived from the motions of the earth and the heavenly bodies; on these lines, first used to place altars, were temples subsequently raised, so uniformly in all succeeding time, and throughout every region of the earth, that it has not entered into the mind of man to inquire into the motive, or to think even of the fact. The process may be seen practised to-day as originally devised, by every Brahmin who prepares the scene for a Sraddha: he commences by drawing the figure of the cross.

The ancestors having attended and taken their seats, they are furnished with water to drink, with water for purification, with water for bathing. They are also clothed.* The food is then presented (through the fire), and they are thus addressed : —

"Ancestors, rejoice ! take your respective shares, and be strong as bulls."

Nor was it from any portion of the hand that they would accept their food ; it had to be presented by the part between the thumb and the forefinger, which afterwards, in Cheiromancy, was known as "the line of life," and which, consequently, was designated *Pitriya.*

After they have fed, the performer of the sacrifices dismisses them with the same honours with which they had been received and thus addresses them : —

"Fathers, to whom food belongs, guard our food, and the other things offered by us ; venerable and immortal as ye are, and conversant with holy truths ; quaff the sweet essence, be cheerful, and depart contented by the paths which gods travel."‡

According to the Institutes of Menu, the first offerings specified are " grains, the *natural product of the earth.*" If this be the commonest of things, it is the first fruits of human toil, and consequently the first of human offerings. Next to these come " vegetables, rice, clarified butter, the milk of cows, and food made from it ; but flesh is particularly agreeable to them, especially that of the longeared white goat."

The cow is not mentioned by the Hindu lawgiver, but that it had been anciently sacrificed, the name of the yearly Sraddha shows ; and still a cow, after having been consecrated as a victim is liberated in their honour. Honey and milk § are specified

* The nearest relation presents a woollen yarn, and, naming the deceased, says, "May this apparel, made of woollen yarn, be acceptable to thee!" A thread is placed on each funeral cake, to serve as apparel for the manes, and each time the same words are repeated : "Fathers! apparel is offered unto you."—*As. Res.,* v. vii., p. 268.

† The hand was divided into four pure parts ; the little finger was Caya ; the root of the thumb belonged to Brahma ; the tips of the fingers to the gods in general, and dipped in the Tritham, or holy water, for the sprinking of all offerings.

‡ Δάιψõνων αναγρφή.

§ " The milk of animals, with undivided hoofs, of a camel, a ewe, or a deer or a buffalo, is unfit for ancestral oblations."—*Vishnu Purana*, p. 333.

as their food of predilection ; but, " whatever suitable food is presented with pure faith, and with the enunciation of *name or race* to ancestors, at an obsequial oblation, becomes food to them."

These different aliments supply to the ancestors satisfaction of various degrees of intensity and duration; their gratification depended however, not only on the quality of the offering, but also on the appositeness of the occasion. The malignant spirits being always at war among the stars with the beneficent ones, seeking to disturb the order of nature, and thereby to destroy the progeny of men, the successful accomplishment of the various phases of the Heavenly Host had to be celebrated as triumphs, on which the ancestors, as parties concerned, had to be congratulated : such as the new moon,* the 15th of the moon's wane, the new year, solar and lunar eclipses, certain lunations of the dark fortnights, the solstices, and when the sun is in Aries.‡

The following is the song of the Pitris, heard by Ikshwaku, the son of Menu, in the groves of Kalápa (skirts of the Himalaya) :—

" Those of our descendants shall follow a righteous path, who shall reverently present us with cakes at Gaya. May he be born in our race who shall give us, on the thirteenth of Bhádrapada and Mágha, milk, honey, and clarified butter." §

There are two classes of rites; those performed by the offering of the cake, and those by the libation of water. The last class in the failure of males could be performed by females; the

---

* " The Pitris derive satisfaction for eight years from ancestral offerings upon the day of new moon, when the star of the conjunction is Anuradha, Visakha, or Swati ; and for twelve years, when it is Pushya, Ardra, or Punarvasu. It is not easy for a man to effect his object, who is desirous of worshipping the Pitris, or the gods, on a day of new moon, when the stars are those of Dhanishthá Purvabhadrapada, or Satabhisha."—*Vishnu Purana*, p. 322.

† The dark half of the month, the dark asterisms and signs, belonged to the Pitris and ancestors ; the bright ones, to the gods.

‡ This point deserves to be examined by astronomers, as possibly affording some indication of the date of this institution ; if, indeed, it may be supposed to have reference to the commencement of the year, with the sun in that sign.

§ Vishnu Purana, p. 333.

others by daughters' sons and their sons, and also by the "prince who inherits the deceased's property." *

The ceremony, however, did not solely consist in feeding the ancestors; their honour required the distribution of food to the living, and chiefly to the indigent and destitute; it was equally furnished to animals and men: thus the connexion of the living child with the dead parent was used to inculcate practices of charity. In process of time the Brahmins were not neglected, and this seems to have constituted a chief source of their sustenance; arrogating to themselves the office of fire, what was given to them, satisfied the ancestors.

This support could only be received from those who were bound by affinity to offer it. Deprived of it they were emaciated with want,† and disturbed with sorrow. Some wild, indefinite, and supernatural torments—some incomprehensible fate—fell upon them and awaited them; and they "blasted with their sighs" the mansions of those who refused them their rites. Whoever was guilty of this dereliction was exposed to the most terrible punishments on earth, being, *ipso facto*, excommunicated, and so cut off from his fellow-men, that his touch polluted, and the very sight of him defiled the eye.‡

The Pitris had, however, effectual means of control over their descendants. If they could blast and curse, they could also bless and cause to fructify. To them imploration was made for success in every enterprise, and acknowledgments offered in return for good fortune. Vows were paid to them for fame, wealth, power, length of days, or increase of happiness. They are applied to as *intercessors*,§ both for men on earth and for

---

* Vishnu Purana, p. 318.

† Thus the gods of Greece and Rome lived on the adoration of men; therefore the lamentation of the queen of the gods :—

   —— "Quisquis numen Junonis adorat

   Preterea, aut supplex aris imponat honorem?"

‡ Whoever looked on him had to stop and fix his eyes upon the sun, that by its rays his sight might be purified ; whoever was touched by him, had to rush into the water with his clothes on, to escape from the defilement.

§ At the Sapindana, or last obsequies for one recently deceased, is uttered this prayer :—

"By (the intercession of) those souls, who are mine by affinity, who are

departed spirits, and they stood in the relation to men, of saints and of gods, linked to them by the ties of blood, so that each race of mortals on earth became part of a dynasty in heaven ; the gods were not brought down to the level of the Pitris, but these were raised to the rank of divinities. As fire was worshipped as their messenger,* so was the moon as their abode.

"May this oblation to fire, which conveys offerings to the manes, be efficacious."

"May this oblation to the moon, wherein the progenitors of mankind abide, be efficacious."

The gods are introduced into the ceremonies of the Pitris, not these into those of the gods. "Two cushions are placed one on each side of the altar for the gods, and six for the ancestors before it."

Of the twelve species of Sraddhas,† one (the tenth) is "Sraddha, in honour of deities." Another (the ninth) is preparatory to any solemn rite, and considered a part of it. The two last are as *propitiatory for a journey*, or to *sanctify a meal of flesh*. In fact, the Sraddha serves all the purposes of religion; and the rites to the gods and the ancestors were so assimilated as to be performed in common.‡ But the line between duty to the ancestors, consisting in the furnishing of food, and duty to the gods by a virtuous life, is altogether effaced by a remarkable notion that the Pitris were fed by the moon's light, which accounted for the changes in that luminary ; and when the reservoir was exhausted it had to be replenished by the good deeds of men ; so that the nightly changes of the sky, in connexion with their ancestral reverence, became an unceasing incitement to a good

animated (shades), who have reached a common abode, who have accordant minds, may prosperity be mine in this world for a hundred years !"—*As. Res.*, vol. vii., p. 267.

* In the sacrifice, the clarified butter seems the offering to fire itself. When the gods performed the sacrifice by which the world is created, it is said, "spring was the butter, summer the fuel, and sultry weather the oblation."

† *Nirnaya Sindha*—quoted by Mr. Colebrook.

‡ "Some comprise all the daily sacraments in one ceremony, called Vaisivadeva. It consists in oblations to the gods, to the manes, and to the spirits, out of the food prepared for the daily meal; and in the gift of a part of it to the guests."—*Colebrook.*

life ; and the sustenance of the manes depended no less on obedience than on sacrifice.

Unless by this transition, how, indeed, could the notion of sustaining the gods by sacrifice have ever arisen ? The original conception of the Divinity must, by universal consent, have been that of an incorporeal and all-powerful Creator :* that it was so in Brahminism there is no doubt. If, then, we have the Maker of the Universe suffering from emaciation, attenuated by hunger, and begging for the minutest portion of sacrificial butter, even if no bigger than a pistachio nut (the afflicting condition of Indra, at the time of the Buddhistic reform), it was that the distinction between gods and ancestors had been lost.

There were thus in the origin two thoughts in the breast of man ; the one an incorporeal faith, directed to the Creator ; the other a ceremonial love, devoted to the ancestors. As the one lost its distinctness, the other acquired intensity, and when, if I may so say, an external religion arose, the spirit of the former invested itself in the mantle of the latter.

The beatitude of the manes in heaven being dependent on their descendants on earth, the latter were bound, above all things, to take care that their line should not be interrupted. Three duties were imposed ; the one in respect to the wise, the second in respect to the gods, the third in respect to the ancestors. The first was performed by the study of the Vedas ; the second, by sacrifice ; the third, by begetting a male child. The first could only have been imposed after the composition of the Vedas, and consisted in the knowledge of duties ; the second, as we have seen, was performed at once to the gods and the ancestors, and had been performed to the ancestors before the gods ; so that, in fact, the whole duty of the Hindu was summed up in service to the ancestors ; which insured that first object of primeval legislation—the peopling of the earth. Hence, that

---

* "If I were hungry I would not tell thee, for the world is mine and the fullness thereof."—*Ps.* l. 12.

† The whole of the rituals exhibit man struggling with nature to establish a footing on the surface of the earth. "Oh, earth, be free from thorns, be habitable !"

"There were *few children*, little wealth, much fear, many tigers, and thorns for the feet !"—*Khond Ritual.*

inordinate desire still maintained in all eastern countries for off-spring; hence also the female infanticide so prevalent amongst the hill tribes, as they imagine that their chances of male off-spring are thereby increased. The same practice, though otherwise explained, existed in Sparta.

The childless condition carrying such consequences, provision was made for supplying the deficiencies of nature by a legal process, which we translate "adoption." It will, however, be seen at a glance that this relationship had in their system nothing in common with our word.

The purpose was to engraft on the old stock a new shoot, which had, therefore, not only to be completely united to the one, but entirely dissevered from the other. As in the same operation with trees, the main branch could not be taken, and the sprout to be available required to be young.

The eldest son of a house could not become an adopted child, whatever the poverty or distress of the natural father, whatever the wealth and the power of the adopted one, because his duty was that of the continuation of his own line. The younger son —the object of adoption—could not be taken after his habits were formed, or his affections fixed; as an old branch will not serve for a graft. He had to be taken before his fifth year.* The ceremony was a sacrament, named *Hom*, or Joy, and apparently connected with the Tree of Life *(Hom)*. From that hour, the child knows no father but his adopted one; *passes the barrier of Caste;* and succeeds of right to his property. This is required to confirm the adoption, for otherwise he cannot offer to him the Sraddha after his death.

Amongst us, the childless possessor of wealth is incapacitated from disposing of it in a manner which would secure to him even that amount of respect and affection which we still associate with parental and filial ties; and consequently we would imagine that by rendering final the disposal of the property, he would lose those services and that consideration which we look to obtain by

---

* The Hindu lawyers are not decided whether adoption be not valid up to the eighth year; but this is clearly an extension introduced under circumstances which were no longer those of the original institution. This remark dispenses me from entering into the discussion of other points of apparent discrepancy with the view of the case which I here present.

uncertainty of expectation. By this process, as well as by the concurrent habits and feelings, all these ends are attained, and fortune enables a man to supply the niggardliness of nature, securing at once a son to himself and a line of succession to his house.

Shall we treat such a system as rude? Shall we brand it as superstitious? Shall we hold it to have its origin in accident and caprice? Here there may be superstition, but it has been handled with wisdom, and applied with art. In the earliest of laws are anticipated the last conclusions of science; in the first of societies are excluded the principal causes of the breaking up of states. Instituted prior to Caste, it has overruled even its authority.

Other legislations have *reckoned* the family the unit of the state; this *establishes* it. Other systems have looked to preventing public crimes; this, to the nurturing of domestic affections.

It may well be imagined how incomprehensible was such a system to western conquerors—what difficulties it occasioned them when they sought to do right—what facilities it afforded them when they intended to do wrong! It may well be imagined how, in the one case and in the other, the heart of a whole people could be sickened with disgust, or aroused in indignation, by acts which presented to the dispassionate or conscientious observer or judge at home no character of offence.

Of this we have an instance in the case of the late Raja of Sattara, the deprivation of whose property vitiated his adoption, and consequently, according to his belief and that of his fellow-countrymen, consigned his soul to eternal damnation.* The adopted son was placed in the same predicament, being cut off from both stocks. This was the great wrong which he suffered; which all India felt; which no man in England could comprehend; and which, from the incompatibility of ideas, no one belonging to the one country could render intelligible to the people of the other.

Had this happened under a Hindu government, the case would

---

* We have accepted adoption as a legal act, without comprehending its religious bearing; and therefore without perceiving its political consequences. Consult the Gentoo code, and the legal essay of Sir Francis Mc Naughten, although in the first the name does not occur, and to the second the whole matter is unintelligible.

have been provided for; in the event of succession by the prince, for confiscation is wholly prohibited by their law, he was bound to appoint the proper officer to perform in his name the Sraddha, and could only hold the property on that condition. No doubt under the Mussulman system, as it always conformed to existing usages, provision had been made for similar contingencies; an eastern people could not be ignorant of usage, far less contemptuous of it; and though Islam has put an end to the ancestral oblation, the professors of that creed retained its impress in all their ideas,* and in many of their customs.

I have not alluded to the merits of the case; but how much is the character of the penalty aggravated in the mind of the people of India, who know, if we do not, what England owes to the act of this prince, and what had been his devotion to her. What worse fate can England's foes experience? What is to be gained by being her friend? That one Englishman may become surreptitiously rich, the fountain of justice is polluted, and an empire endangered.

That the Sraddha did not originate in the Hindu system is evident from the contradiction in which it stands to caste, to which it must have been anterior; and, further, from its incompatibility with transmigration, which, though in dogma directly opposed to it, has not prevailed against it. They have, further, the tradition of the introduction of this dogma, which is attributed to several personages, but especially to Pururavas, son of Buddha, chief of the Lunar Line, a line marked throughout by religious innovation, and presenting, if not the fleshly body, at least the "ferver" of Buddhism.

We must naturally look to the names as furnishing further elucidation. *Ekkodishto*, the monthly oblation, does not sound by any means Sanscrit; the Zend, however, may aid us. Kuds and Kuddus is the name anciently given to Jerusalem, and still preserved; Feridoun conferred it on a religious edifice which he there constructed. The great annual oblation is called *Sapindana;* in this the cow is consecrated for sacrifice; and here Sanscrit philologists are entirely at fault. In Turkish, *dana* is "cow;" it

---

* In consequence of the childless condition of so many of our countrymen, their disregard of marriage, and indifference as to offspring, we are considered by the Hindus as ignoble, and rated below the lowest outcast.

is the common word in use in every field, market-place, and butcher's shop.* If so, we have then a compound term. *Sapin* is not Turkish; but if we write the word *Sab-i-dana*, we have, in Turkish, "the master and cow."†

Swadha is the word ceremoniously pronounced during the oblation; it means "food," but the Hindus render it "oblation;" and they personified it as the daughter of the patriarch Packshu, and the wife of the Pitris. *Swaha* is "the consuming power of sacrificial fire," which they personify as the sister of the former, and make the wife of *Vahni*, "the god of fire." *Sraddha* itself is in like manner a sister of the other two, and the wife of *Dharma*, "the lord of righteousness." In Sanscrit it is rendered "faith." Had it originally had this meaning, it could never have been given to any ceremony in particular. It follows, then, that the word was foreign, and the rite imported at a time when there existed no abstract idea of faith. Now, in the cuneiform we have the *Thrada*, and it applies to this ceremony; the Sanscrit word is, therefore, adopted from the Zend, with the addition of an " s," as we have already seen in the conversion of *tepe* into *stupa*.

The philosophical character of the Chinese places in a clear light an institution which the legendary, metaphorical, and metaphysical spirit of the Hindus has disguised with fable, and enveloped in mystery. There it is assumed to be the foundation of doctrine, and the political bond of the constitution. What is left to inference and interpretation in India, is in China declared as maxim, and asserted as truth; for instance, " A child serves the dead parents as if they were alive." "The want of posterity is the greatest of defects." " The only act worthy of being esteemed great, is the rendering due service to the dead." " All virtue and all wisdom resides in reverence for elders and parents."

---

* In Sanscrit, Dhenu is " cow," but the exact Turkish word is preserved in the title of the rite.

† Sab is not at present in use by itself, but we have it in *Ev-sab*, "master of the house." *Zabit* is " governor;" the word is supposed to be taken from the Arabs; but it is one of those words which the Arabs themselves have taken from the Zend. It is in common use all over India, in this same sense; but the construction in Sapindana is Turkish, not Sanscrit (gopandana).

That reverence towards the living was maintained by the influence of this ceremonial towards the dead.

We have seen with what pomp the Sraddha was inaugurated or restored under the Hya. At an interval of forty-five centuries it has lost nothing of its grandeur; it is thus described as actually practised :—

"According to the ritual which regulates the state proceedings of the Emperor of China, he is bound to visit every year, on the first day of the first moon, the temple of his ancestors, and to prostrate himself before the tablet of his fathers. There is before the entrance to this temple a long avenue, wherein the tributary princes, who have come to Peking to render homage to the Emperor, assemble. They range themselves right and left of the peristyle, in three lines, each occupying the place appertaining to his dignity : they stand erect, grave, and silent. It is said to be a fine and imposing spectacle, to witness all these remote monarchs attired in their silk robes, embroidered with gold and silver, and indicating, by the variety of their costumes, the different countries they inhabit, and the degrees of their dignity."*

In one respect, however, they failed in philosophy, as compared with the Hindus—they wailed and lamented ; grief was not with Roman stoicism† forbidden, it was indulged in, cultivated, and exhibited ; it was a luxury, a passion, and a performance.‡ The period of mourning lasted for three years, during which time the son was incapacitated for public functions, sometimes dwelling at the entrance of the tomb, and there serving the dead as if yet living.§

---

* Huc's Tartary, v. i., p. 226.

† "What more absurd," nevertheless, asks Cicero, "what more base or deformed, than to place in the station of gods, and to worship with their honour, men swept away by death, and to whom all future service consists in grief ?"

‡ "Those present at the funeral (on the third year after the death) were very much satisfied with the consternation painted on his countenance (the son's), and the violence of his groans."—*Meng Tseu.*

§ This circumstance may countenance the explanation formerly offered by M. Maillot (see Savary's Egypt) of the *Souperails,* by which the mortuary chamber of the Pyramid communicated with the exterior, and opened to the lower portion of the edifice. He imagined that living persons had been entombed with the dead body, and nourished by food transmitted

While the religion of Hoangti anticipated Brahminism in date, the detailed practices, as recorded so far back as the times of the Hya, exactly correspond with those of the present Tartars under their tents. In the "earliest antiquity," the body was cast out into the ditches by the wayside; it is actually exposed by the Tartars on the hill-tops. The number of sacrificial vessels used by the Emperors was nine. The same number is daily used by every Mogul,* and the oblations made therewith by the votaries of Buddha are identical with those prescribed in the Brahmin ritual. I have already referred to the Chinese vases, so to say the earliest coinage, and the most ancient of continuous records; costly in their material, elaborate in their workmanship, beautiful in their forms, and necessarily devoted to the then highest objects of worship; they were sacrificial.† Four emblems are to be found on them—the MOON, the FISH, the EYE, and the CROSS. The two first are united in one of the most ancient; the third appears on nearly all; the last is often repeated, and in various forms.

We have already seen that the moon was the abode of the ancestors; we, therefore, perfectly understand its introduction as an emblem on an ancestral vase, without adopting the explanation offered of moon-worship, The fish and the eye are easily explained in the same manner. The first lived in the element of which the moon's substance was held to be a concretion.

The eye presents us with a point of greater intricacy; and to which belong a multiplicity of interesting ramifications. Whoever has visited the Mediterranean, has observed it painted on the bow of boats and galleys, as it was on those of the Phœnicians of old. It was, amongst the Jews, *enclosed in a triangle,* —an emblem of the Deity. There is a species of Etruscan vase, which has not been understood; on it also are two great eyes.

---

through the aperture so long as any survived to receive it. There are traces of the same practice among the Parsees.

* "Nine copper vases, of the size and form of our liquor glasses, are symmetrically arranged before Buddha. It is in these small chalices that the Tartars daily make to their idol offerings of water, milk, butter, and meal."—*Huc's Tartary.*

† At length a monument of Menes has been discovered in Egypt, and it is unique. It is a gold vase.

It is figured in gigantic proportions on the exterior of the Chaitiyas of the Buddhists; now we discover it in China, on the oldest monuments. The character of those monuments, and the other emblems with which it is associated, point at once to the ancestral worship, itself (as we have seen) the origin of all forms of worship.

The Eye, from its transparent nature in the body, from its connexion with light, would naturally be one of the first of symbols employed by an allegorising faith; but we must find some minute point of identification to connect it with the manes; and it appears to me that that is afforded in the consecration of the hare* by the Chinese, the cat by the Egyptians, and the rabbit by the Greeks. We have seen of what importance in the ancestral worship was the increase and decrease of the moon. This was supposed to be typified in the dilation and contraction of the iris in these animals; if they were accepted as emblems of the moon, how much more the eye itself? There was not only the "lunar eye," which expressed duty, but the "solar eye," with a more general significance, conveying benevolence. Thus the Brahmin prays, "May all beings view me with the eye of the sun. I view all beings with the solar eye. Let us view each other with the solar eye." The eye was also the visible sign of grief, and thus we have among the Egyptians the eye and the *tear;* the right eye being supposed to represent the sun; the left, the moon.

The Jews placed the eye in the triangle: now, the triangle is connected, though in a manner which I do not understand, with the Sraddha, for it was one of the forms of the earth-elevation or altar constructed for that purpose. It was a square in ordinary cases; but for a person recently deceased, and apparently during the season of mourning, it *was a triangle.*

---

* This festival, known as the *Yué-Ping* (Loaves of the Moon), dates from the remotest antiquity. Its original purpose was to honour the moon with superstitious rites. On this solemn day, all labour is suspended; the workmen receive from their employers a present of money; every person puts on his best clothes; and there is a merrymaking in every family. Relations and friends interchange cakes of various sizes, on which is stamped the image of the moon; that is to say, a *Hare* crouching amid a small group of trees."—*Huc's Tartary*, vol. i., p. 61.

It is impossible not to suspect here that that great mystery of the Trinity, which pervades all Eastern religions, was itself connected with the ancestral sacrifice. How else explain the use of this remarkable figure, which has ever continued to be its emblem ? To this we must join the triple division of Fire, essentially belonging to the same worship. The Chinese defined the Deity as "Trinity in Unity, and Unity in Trinity." This doctrine, it will be self-evident, has no connexion whatever with the Trinity of the Brahmins, or the Trinity of the Buddhists, which had reference to attributes, combination, or time ; being the "Creator, Preserver, and Destroyer ;" "Wisdom, Nature, and Union ;" and "Past, Present, and Future ;" whilst its original form on the eastern limits of the old continent exactly corresponds with the specification of the Athanasian creed, being the three Hypostases, or Impersonations of one and the same divine nature.

If we are to accept this as a record of primitive revelation, all inquiry is at an end, and all argument ceases ; but if we are to consider it in a mere human sense, that is to say, as a doctrine evolved by the unaided effort of the spirit of man, then must we proceed as in respect to any other phenomenon. Now, as in our own faith, the doctrine of the Trinity confessedly transcends reason it is hopeless to look for the origin of it in the Chinese; that is to say, if we consider it as a conclusion arrived at with reference to the nature of the Deity ; but there is a path which we may take, and proceeding by which we may find the problem less intractable.

The primitive conception of God must have been one of such profound reverence, that to dare to inquire into his nature would have been deemed sacrilege. In the words of Menu, he could be "apprehended only in the *class* of Abstraction." He was without form, without limit, *without name.* How, then, could he be divided into THREE *Persons ?* In fact, that Materialism which produced Polytheism sprung from the deep abstraction connected with the idea of a Creator. It may, therefore, be inferred, looking at the matter in a human point of view, that the doctrine of the Trinity, as regarded the Godhead, was not primitive, but derivative.

Whence then could it have sprung? From Psychology.

Death, though a mystery, did not repel, it invited, inquiry; the nature of death could be comprehended only by that of life. "What is God?" is a question which no primitive man would ask. "What am I?" is one which must ever have been present to his thoughts. Suppose, now, that the answer made had been by a division of the soul into different natures, and these threefold, would we not have, as regards human life, three in one and one in three? If so answered in respect to the life of man, the idea of a Trinity of Spirit was established in his mind, and might thereafter be applied to other spiritual existences, and even to the Divine Nature itself.

This is no hypothesis; we have this very division of Life a fundamental dogma amongst those populations to whom I have repeatedly referred as preserving the earliest records of religious thoughts and ceremonies. The Khonds say that life is composed of three souls, one of which is animal, one intellectual, and one Divine; that the first, when the body dies, dies with it; that the second after death is punished, or recompensed, according to the body's deeds; and that the third returns to and is absorbed in the Deity, from which it had originally emanated.*

An ampler conception of life and existence has not been attained to by all subsequent metaphysics; extending immortality backwards, and separating the taint of earth from the breath of Heaven; and in it we may recognise conjoined the elements of the several dogmas, on which are based the various structures of philosophy, belief, and superstition.†

---

* Macpherson's "Religion of the Khonds."

Lydus de mensibus, indicates this threefold life: the First, the Spark of Life; the Second, Divine Breath; the Third, Holy Love.

† Greek philosophy is multiform, and no common rule can be laid down for any belief, but the Greek tongue has for the soul three names—ψυχη, φρην, and θυμος, conveying the idea of distinct existences, united indeed in life, but separated at death. Homer represents the θυμος of Hercules conversing with Ulysses in Hades, whilst his φρην is making love above to Hebe. The Romans, always closer to the Himalaya than the Greeks, had explicitly and universally the tripartite division of *Manes, Anima,* and *Umbra:* the first on separation descended to Tartarus or Elysium; the second ascended to its source, the elemental fire; the third hovered round the tomb.

The point upon which I rest here, is that this Trinity was connected with the soul of man, and therefore with the ancestral oblation; that with it, too, was connected the figure of the Triangle, especially applied at the time when the separation was supposed to take place by the occurrence of death.

It was only in the fourth century, and after the Labarum of Constantine had appeared in the skies, that the Christian Church adopted the cross as an emblem: it was centuries later that the cruciform cathedral came into use, through the Goths of Spain and the Saracens of Africa, whose architecture was adopted from the Philistine tribes of Barbary. The Chaitiya of the Buddhists, in all the completeness still to be witnessed in the rock-temples of India, was then inaugurated in Europe, as at once the Gothic and Christian architecture.

If it be repugnant to all our notions to assert that the cross, as a Christian emblem, did not originate in the crucifixion, so is it perplexing to our erudition to find it a religious emblem before that event, and an object of veneration and adoration through all the regions of the earth and from the earliest times.

The Cross was known to the Jews; Moses raised the serpent on a cross in the Desert; Christ refers to it as an emblem of persecution. On the two earliest monuments of China, we have that cross, which is called "Greek;" and also one with a longer limb—that called "Latin." * In the hieroglyphics the cross appears on the breast of the tribes of Northern Asia, 1500 years before the crucifixion.† It is tattooed on those of the Breber tribes of Africa, as it was on those of the tribes of North America, in whose tombs it was also found; and who adored it when presented to them by the Spaniards.‡ It appears

---

* See vases of the Shang Dynasty, *J As. Soc.*, v. i.

† "The adoption of the last" (a small cross *suspended to a necklace*) "was not peculiar to them (the Sharu); it was also appended to or figured upon the robes of the Rot-'n-no; and traces of it may be seen in the fancy ornaments of the Rebo, showing that it was already in use as early as the 15th century, before the Christian era."—*Sir G. Wilkinson's Ancient Egyptians*, vol. i., page 376.

‡ The Indians not only knew, but adored, the cross, which made the Spaniards imagine it was a delusion of the devil, and invent various other solutions of the mystery.—*Harrera las Indeas occ.*, dec. 11, l. iii., c.

in the Buddhistic monuments of India,* and the coins called
Hindu-Scythic, and amongst the stamps by which the tribes of
Tartary marked their horses.† In one of the last discovered
Assyrian monuments it hangs on the breast of a king, exactly
in the form and fashion of a modern decoration.

The only explanation which has been offered for the paramount
importance of this figure, is that it typified the four elements and
the four cardinal points; but the elements were five, not four, as
amongst them was enumerated the empyrean, or *Αιθηρ, because*
the points of the cross are five, not four; nor was it necessary to
typify what itself was the point of adoration.

All the sacred buildings of antiquity were most rigidly mathe-
matical in their form, and astronomic in their position. They are
composed of the circle, the oval, the square, the parallelogram,
and the cross. The circle belongs to the worship of fire, and we
are familiar with it in the beautiful temple of Vesta at Rome, and
in the majestic Pantheon, originally a fire temple, but restored
and disfigured by Agrippa by the addition of the colonnade. The
Dagopas were also round, which I take, however, to be only a
modification of the square pyramid. In every case the ground
plan presents the circle enclosed within a square. To the building
so modified, they gave the shape of a bell, evidently in connexion with the figure of the lotus, and with the " sacred bell,"
itself, so essential an instrument in their worship.

The oval represented the figure of the elliptic. The examples
of it are rare.

The square structures are both monumental, as in the Dagopa
and the pyramids of Egypt, and ecclesiastical, as in the pagoda;
and are invariably placed according to the cardinal points.

In the Pagoda and in the Chaitiya the square becomes extended to the oblong and to the Cross. I give a description of
one from Tavernier, which will further exhibit the still closer

* From this is derived the ornament which we call "Etruscan," and
which is equally found in the earliest monuments of Egypt and of China.
" The Swastica is found on most Buddhist coins from all parts of India
It is also met with, initial, terminal, or both, on Buddhist inscriptions at
Junia, Karli, and in Kuttech.—*J. As. Soc.*, v. vi., p. 454.

† See plates appended to Levchin's Kirgiz Kazaks.

approach to the Catholic form of worship in his day ; it is the celebrated pagoda of Casi or Benares. "It is placed on the bank of the Ganges, into which a flight of stone steps descends from the gate of the pagoda. The body of the temple itself is constructed in the form of a VAST CROSS, with a very high cupola in the centre of the building, but somewhat pyramidal towards the summit ; and at the extremity of each of the four parts of the Cross is a tower, with an ascent on the outside, and balconies at stated distances, affording delightful views of the city, the river, and adjacent country. Under the high dome, in the middle, there stands an altar, in form of a table, eight feet in length, and six in breadth, covered sometimes with rich tapestry, and sometimes with cloth of gold or silver, according to the greater or less solemnity of the festival. Upon this altar were several idols, one of which, six feet in height, had its neck splendidly decorated with a chain of precious stones, of which the priests have a variety for different festivals, some of rubies, some of pearls, and others of emeralds. The head and neck of this idol were alone visible ; all the rest of the body was covered with an embroidered robe, spreading in ample folds upon the altar below." *

The Pagoda of Seringham recalls Ecbatana. Mr. Orme describes it as composed "of seven square enclosures, one within the other, the walls of which are twenty-five feet high, and four thick. These enclosures are 350 feet distant from one another, and each has four large gates, with a high tower, which are placed, one in the middle of each side of the enclosure, and opposite to the *four cardinal points*. The outward wall is near four miles in circumference." †

The systematic regularity of those buildings shows the deep importance that was attached to the position of the worshipper, and which we are naturally to expect in religions which saw in the heavenly bodies animated intelligences, considered the firmament to be tenanted by countless numbers of spiritual beings endowed with terrible and Divine power, as also by maleficent spirits almost equally gifted, and in whose struggles the fate of

---

* Voyage, iv., p. 149. See particularly Furgusson's "Rock Temples of India."

† Orme's Hist. of Indostan, vol. i., p. 178.

man was involved, where the preponderance of the benign over
the maleficent influences, though daily in the balance, was
necessary to ensure the order of nature, and the existence of the
universe. Even without a celestial belief, or a Divinatory Code,
we see faiths and institutions threatened by the revolving
motions of a priest round an altar table.

Under these impressions, not only the plan of the Temple, but
the respective positions of host and guest, &c.,were subject to astronomic conditions. In every daily ceremony, the different points
of the Heavens had to be turned to or avoided, according to
their various influences, or symbolical applications. The Arhan
and the Brahmin, the Yogi and the Sudra, had equally at every
moment, and in every incident, to mark the divisions of the
compass with a steersman's accuracy.*

Amongst the various religions which have sprung from Tartary,
the fundamental points are much the same; yet we find a
striking difference in the direction of worship. The sun is
more particularly the object of adoration to the Fire worshippers
than to the Brahmins; but the former being a reformation
directed against the latter, the Kibla was immediately changed
together with the rectangular form of the building. The circle
was substituted for the square, the point of adoration was placed
on the south, and the entrance on the north.

The Brahmins placed the great entrance to the east, in order
that the morning rays should break upon the sanctuary. The
worshippers having performed their ablutions before dawn crowd
round the portals, which are thrown open the moment the sun
appears ; the temple, indeed, opens on the four sides, but the gates

---

* An Emperor of China is confused and disturbed when he perceives his
father looking towards him, "with his face to the south." Amongst the
Chinese it was the designation of a heinous offence " to dig into an eastern .
wall," the women's apartments being on that side. A man inflicting the
punishment of death upon himself in expiation of a crime, after having
received the wound, had to step towards the south; the bed had to be
placed north-east and south-west. Paternal ancestors had to be worshipped with their faces to the north, the maternal with their faces to the
east. A recent theory has established new Hygeian rules for the position
of the bed in reference to the rotation of the earth, but this is as old as
the hills, or—Menu. In his Institutes the sanitary point for the head of the
bed is north-west, and for the feet south-east.

to the east predominated. That the Jews had a difference to mark is shown by the point of adoration being transferred to the *west*, and in a minor degree to the north.

Abraham, on Mount Moriah, turned to the west. The Holy of Holies was placed at the west end. In the vision of Ezekiel (ch. viii.) the vengeance of God is denounced against the Apostate Jews, who had "their back towards the temple of the Lord, and WORSHIPPED THE SUN *towards the east.*" Christianity, making its difference with Judaism, removed back again its Kibla to the east.* The Reformation signified its protest by placing the priest on the *north* of the altar.† The Dissenters, like the early Christians, pay no attention to the points of the compass, but the new sect in the Anglican church go round again to the east.

If, then, the professors of a religion which pretends to be spiritual, and in which the turning to the east has been forbidden, because it implies "worship of the sun," and who are, moreover, assured of the immaterial being of their Maker, and his Omnipresence, are thus to be traced in their mutations by imaginary astronomic lines, how much more must they have been important in religions professedly astronomic, and wherein the meditation upon mere geographical points constituted a large portion of their devotion.

But, whatever the point which might have been particularly or successively preferred, they all equally depended upon the accuracy of drawing the intersecting lines. Whatever the object of varying adoration, the plan itself was connected with that original form of worship out of which the various beliefs subsequently sprang; and in fact, among the earliest on record we find one which especially bore the designation of "Religion of the Cross," which prevailed in China as a reformation of that of Hoang-ti from before the Deluge, to at least the 5th century after Christ.‡ But as this was neither the object of adoration,

---

* This did not, however, occur till late; the early churches were placed without any regard to the points of the compass and were often circular.

† The Rubric and the 82nd canon direct that, "the Table at Communion time shall stand in the body of the Church, or in the chancel, and that the priest shall stand at the north side of the Table."

‡ Fa Hian mentions the assembling from all parts of the "Sectaries of the

nor the name of a founder, it must have been the introduction of a ceremony, and not that of a belief; that ceremony, the drawing of the cross, is preliminary throughout Hindustan to this hour to the performing of the Sraddha:* thus the cross became the emblem of the ancestral worship.

This operation of drawing the Cross is identical with that of the Etruscan augur, when drawing the Cardo and crossing it with the Decumanus, in order to describe the bounds for sacred edifices. The very word cardo is derived from the Zend, and signifies adoration; and amongst the Chinese the mere act of forming the figure of the cross was so esteemed:† to this idea no doubt we must refer the turning-wheels of the Buddhists, which were originally in the form of a cross. The universality of its adoption from Rome to China, from the Druids to the Mexicans, who worshipped it when presented to them by the Spaniards, proves alike its high antiquity and its use in that lofty and central region to which in so many other points the diverging lines of superstition and belief have severally to be traced back.

But wherein lay the association with the worship of the ancestors? It lay in the necessity of fixing a point for the sacrifice. This sacrifice was not made at the tomb; there was neither grave, nor funeral pyre; the body was disregarded and cast out; there were then no temples; there was no one spot more consecrated than another; the Pitris belonged to the stars which they were supposed to inhabit; the lines of the heaven were, therefore, to be brought down upon the earth, and the intersection of the *Red Line* of Fire, with the *Yellow Line* of earth, determined by the points of the compass, was supposed to be the fitting place to invoke them down.

Once thus associated it necessarily took hold on the imaginations and affections of men, as implying a knowledge of the deep mysteries of the Universe, as the connecting link with the

cross," to celebrate in Thibet the great quinquennial festival of the Buddhists; the same as the *Ti* of the Chinese.

* See description by Colebrooke, *As. Res.*, vol. vii.

† Hien yuen "joined together two pieces of wood, crossing each other to honour the very High, and was thence called Hien Yuen, for the cross piece is called Hien, and the straight one from north to south Yuen."— *Shan King.*

Invisible. It was, in fact, in matters of faith, what the compass was to the mariner, pointing to them the way of salvation. It was consecrated to their ruling passion, ancestral devotion, and filial piety; and then there was a world largely stocked with affections and rich in love. No wonder that religion received from it a name, and that the emblem has spread to every clime.

. I had omitted one point, not to encumber the matter with details, which I now advert to for its argumentative value. Besides food and raiment, the ancestors required drink, and water for ablution. Fire did not, however, serve for conveying water. It was besides an element, and constituted the substance of the gods. They had recourse to a peculiar process; it was *suspended*,[*] or poured out, and so supposed to be conveyed to them. Probably *motion* was given to it; this the wave-offering of the Jews would suggest. They used fire, and sacred fire. The vessel used in sacrifice by the Hindus is called Argo Nauta. In the Jewish sacrifice the vessel used for receiving the blood was called Aganath.[†]

Amongst the Brahmins and the Buddhists the Cross is known as *Swastika*, thus: ⌐⌐   It was in this very form that it was first adopted by the Christians.[‡]   I subjoin some of the

---

[*] Milk is suspended together with the water. In some mystic manner milk was associated with the elements. "The waters in heaven, in the atmosphere, and on earth, have been united with milk." The " path by which the gods travel " is supposed to be the Milky Way.

[†] Exod. xxiv., 6.

[‡] This was the figure in the mythology of the north, to which we have given the name of " *Thor's Hammer*," and which is explained as the Thunderbolt. The first appearance of the Cross in this form amongst the Christians has taxed the ingenuity of Von Hammer, whilst it has exhausted his learning. He explains it as a conjunction of four letters G in Greek, to stand for knowledge "four times repeated." Müller thus notices both:—

" Occurit denique in monumentis Christianis forma crûcis   ⌐⌐   Bold.

351, 352; Lupi p. 11 in vestitu fossoris cujus figuram pictam exhibet d'Agincourt fasc. III. tab. xii. 1; quam Hammerus mysticam quoque perhibet, quadruplex Γ initium vocis γνῶσις ea contineris tatuens (p. 94). Quæ vero figura, cum apud Japanos quoque inveniatur Deo Xaïa sacca (Georgi

forms in which it appears on the vases of the Hya and the Shang dynasties, cotemporaneous with Noah.

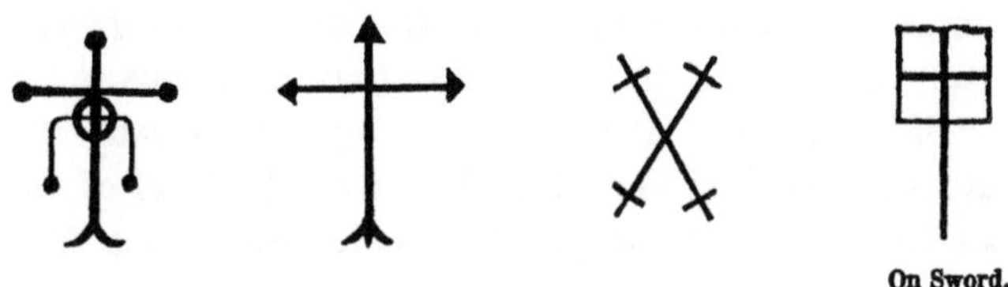

The first letter of the Chinese Alphabet is a Cross in this form :   Their writing being originally ideographic, it is explained as implying " a home, a *temple*, or a niche for an idol. It was anciently an ornament for a temple."*   On the early Chinese vases this figure   is used to enclose distinguished names, as the oval or cartouche of the Egyptians. The Cross appears also on the sepulchral monuments of the Tartars.

Thus, then, the earliest temples were constructed in the form of a Cross, and the most ancient of those discovered in India are in all points the facsimile of a Gothic cathedral—a form not explained by any inherent use, and referable only to the practice observed in the ancestral worship.

There has been abundance of disquisition on an ancient ornament which we choose to call a "cross." It has suggested learned commentaries and endless explanations, but the *religion* bearing that name has strangely suggested no inquiry.

"The Roman Catholic, or the Greek," says Clarke, "in bowing before the Cross, would be little disposed to believe that centuries before the birth of Christ the same emblem was adored as that of the Resurrection."

Now the figure referred to by the learned traveller is not a cross, nor has it any connexion whatever in its symbolical origin,

Alphab. Tibet, p. 460, 725), neque desideratur in moneta veteri Celtogallica itidemque observatur in monumentis populorum Scandinavorum, amuletis maxime aureis, juxta imaginem Thori, cujus fulmen expressisse videtur, fortuitum hunc diversorum adeo populorum consensum mysticæ cuidam causæ minime tribuendum, sed casui unice adscribendum putaverim."

* *Po koo too.*   Apud As. Soc., vol. i., p. 71.

mythological or national history, with the cross of antiquity.
He is speaking of the *Tau* of the Egyptians, which in its
natural sense was a *key* adapted for the opening of doors, the
turning of sluices, and probably also that ingenious masonic
device for lifting stones. It became the key symbolically of the
womb, and a future life; and thus decorates the hand of Osiris,
as it does in its modern shape the escutcheon of the Roman

Pontifex. This is what is called the *Crux Ansata*, 

being in fact the letter **T** (tau) with a handle. Mysticism in
abundance was evolved from the figure, which I do not enter
into, because it is precisely what I want to put aside in order to
get at the source.

There is another figure of Indian origin which bears to this a
close resemblance, and with which it has, therefore, been confounded, especially as the mysticism which enveloped the one in-
termingled with that which belonged to the other. The Indian
figure may be represented by an anchor without the stocks, thus:

or as a boat and a mast, standing for the *Argo nauta*,

typifying the double generative power of nature. The connexion
with the Tau is obtained by an easy process in argument, that of
reversing it, when it becomes pretty nearly a **T**. In China, however, there is a TI which also is the letter T, but with a perfectly
distinct meaning, and represents the outspread canopy of heaven.
That there could be no real connexion between the Egyptian Tau
and the Hindu *Argo Nauta* appears in this: that the Egyptians
did not entertain the doctrines upon which the latter was
founded; for they separated the Linga and the Yoni, of which it
was the conjoint emblem.

There were thus two cruciform figures and one cross complete; we have confounded them together; we have mixed up
the ideas from which they sprung, and the myths to which they
gave rise. They belong to different nations, to different periods;
they are founded on wholly dissimilar ideas, having different
names, and are of different forms; the Tau rising in Egypt, in
connexion with that people's notions of a future state; the Argo

Nauta rising in the Himalaya, and having reference to the mysteries of life ; beyond these, we come to the figure represented in the configuration of the plateau of Pamer, the primitive abode ot man, called " the cross," typifying the motion of the earth and the heavenly bodies, and employed as the process of consecration, of which it contained the idea.

Wherever we find fire-worship we have found the ancestral worship. The latter is to be held a distinct religion, on which others have been engrafted—not a portion of different creeds ; to this religion, sacrifice was peculiar—fire was its instrument, and the cross its sign.

This is not a theory propounded, but an explanation offered, for as yet no explanation has ever been suggested of *sacrifice*. It has been strangely overlooked that this rite did not consist in the slaughter of the victim, but on its being *laid on the fire*. It was thus it became " sacrifice," being made sacred. *Sacrum faceo:* by that process it was *oblated*, or borne to the gods. Expiation or atonement, the accepted reason of sacrifice, had no connexion with its being burnt. No doubt, both expiation and execration came to be associated with the rite ; but they bear only on the life of the victim, and noways explain the manner of disposing of the body, in which the value of sacrifice depended.

I now come to Iran ; having already referred the name of Sraddha to the Zend, we may expect to find it here more clearly defined, and more distinctly represented than in the other systems. This, however, is not the case. In one point, indeed, it gives us a positive assurance of the lineal derivation of the Parsees, from the old Mahabadians with their proper names and designations ; for in the Zendavesta the enumeration and invocation of the ancestors, which, without the knowledge of this rite, would be set down to mere vague tradition, becomes a record of legal authority ; and these, though with considerable lacunes, they trace back to Jemshid and Cayoumers. I may here remark that the air of fable connected with the latter arises from the supposed etymology of his name as first man (Mesha) ; but the first man of the Parsees is a wholly distinct personage—as much so as Adam and Abraham.

Beyond this we find little in ceremonial or in monuments to illustrate the ceremony, but in the religion itself we have valuable light as bearing on the metaphysical and dogmatic part ; and, in fact, of all the religions of the East that of the Parsees is the most interesting, as being freest from metaphysics and mythology ; as inculcating the purest morals ; and as linking together, in a manner nowhere else to be found, the earliest belief of mankind, not with the maxims only, but with many of the most important doctrines of Christianity. It is reluctantly that I exclude what I had prepared upon this subject, as exceeding the bounds of digression ; I am, therefore, reduced to a mere statement of conclusions ; and I may once for all remark, that I have laboured under considerable embarrassment from the constantly recurring dilemma of excursiveness and repetition. The subject treated of in this volume is linked to so many extraneous matters, whilst the proof has to be reiterated on so many distinct fields, that this dilemma repeats itself at every step ; and whilst seeking, perhaps unsuccessfully, to avoid the one or the other fault, I may have equally fallen into both.

The oblation to the ancestors, or their sustenance, depends upon their being considered as ghosts; for if they passed into another state, either that of judgment, which would allot them a habitation of happiness or of misery, or if they animated other bodies, such oblation would be needless ; yet we have concurrently oblation and transmigration. The question then arises, whether transmigration was the original creed, and the Sraddha the foreign graft, or the reverse.* When, however, a ritual observance is in conflict with a metaphysical conception it is to be inferred that the latter is the ingraft on the former. But we have here the tradition of the introduction of the dogma, together with the explanation of its motive—that of putting an end to bloody sacrifice, whether of man or animals; and though this is understood as simply affecting the condition of the victim, it was no doubt aimed, although it failed in its effect, at the object of the sacrifice ; the sacrifice has been maintained, although the nature of the offering has been altered ; or, more

* " Of the Hindu Triad, or of their progeny in any of the numerous ramifications, they (the hill tribes) have no notion ; and independently of the absence of idols, their disbelief in transmigration plainly shows that, whatever their religion may be, it is not a branch of the Brahminical faith."— *Harkness's Neilgherry Hills,* p. 23.

accurately, brought back to its original form of libation—fruits, flowers, and sweet odours.

Arianism, as we have seen, was a reform of Brahminism; "Given against the Divas," was the title of the sacred writings. They are required to resist the sacrilege of burning, or burying, the body. They devote Indra to execration, and in fact attack the then existing system as directly as the United Colonies attacked the English Parliament, or as the Reformation attacked Catholicism. But Zoroaster lived in the sixth century before Christ, when the Parsees were an oppressed people, enslaved to the Assyrians, and situated at a great distance from India, where at that time the Buddhist reform had prevailed over Indra; besides, the Parsees, when they regained national independence, had to struggle with the tribes and religion of Turan; Zoroaster himself fell a sacrifice to the political power and religious hatred of that race, who for a time prevailed over his country and faith. Thus entirely cut off from India, the Parsees were, moreover, engaged against two powerful enemies, the Assyrians to the west, the Turanians, or (as they are expressly called by the compilers of the Dabistan) Turks,* to the north.

These doctrines must, therefore, have belonged to another epoch, and in fact Zoroaster professes only to restore "the religion of Jemshid," whom we may safely identify with the first Zoroaster, and the connexion is rendered indubitable by the ancestral sacrifice to which I have already referred. We have seen that the Arians were established in India, and there conquered by the Hindus; but as the latter came from Tartary, Brahminism had been there established at a still earlier period, and so was in contact with the Arians on both fields, and during a long period of time. Now the date which, after all the light which has been thrown on chronology, is assigned by the best authority to the origin of the Mahabadian dynasty, is not less than the 23rd century before Christ, admitting a possible margin beyond that period of several centuries, the Oriental writers carrying it up to thirty-seven centuries B. C. We may, therefore, take the Parsee doctrines as a record of the ideas existing about the time of the Deluge, it being then a reform of a still

* So also by Ferdousi, Hamza, and all Oriental writers.

more ancient system, which system is now admitted to date in India from 3102 years B. C.*

But Arianism seems to have been a reform of the religion of Hoang Ti no less than of Brahminism, for it denounces the gravest imaginable penalties against a practice which that religion especially consecrated—that of mourning and lamentation. The Hindus had a "river of hell" (Veitarani) which flowed with the tears of relatives; the Arians carried this river round their Paradise, so as to render it unapproachable by those whose relatives supplied the lugubrious waves: thus was the screaming ghost hurried away to that worst region, appropriated, as in Dante's Hell, to those who had neither virtues to recompense, nor crimes to punish. If this hypothesis be correct, the religion of Hoang Ti must have coexisted with Arianism in Tartary no less than Brahminism, and I have already assigned the grounds on which I have concluded Hoang Ti to have been the title of the Turkish conqueror Ogouz Khan, the seat of whose empire was Kashgar.

Metempsychosis, though it did not prevail against the Sraddha, may have obliterated other doctrines; as, for instance, that of a Final Judgment, the Resurrection in the body, and a Future State of Penalties and Recompenses, with all which it was incompatible, being itself a final judgment, the spirits passing according to their acts into other human bodies, or into those of beasts, or into divine natures; and each of these bodies would have an equal claim to the spirit which had inhabited them. Now the Parsees have a Paradise, a Resurrection in the Body, and a Final Judgment; we may therefore infer that such was the general belief prior to the introduction of metempsychosis. The ideas of the Hill tribes in many points support the conclusion, and traces of the Resurrection are to be found in the notion of the Hindus, of the restoration to the spirit, of the organs that had been destroyed by the funeral pyre.

It would be sufficiently striking to find the doctrines enunciated in Judea by Christ and his disciples, in an Oriental creed. How much more so to discover that they belonged at one time to the whole ancient world. This issue depends on the superior anti-

* See Leipsius's Chronology, p. 2.

quity of the Sraddha to the Metempsychosis; so that, however objectionable the form it may have assumed, the Sraddha is the evidence of the primitive and universal simplicity of faith.

I cannot here omit mentioning one of the most beautiful of allegories which have descended to us from these times. The soul could reach the Paradise of the Arians only by a long narrow bridge. The ghost as he approached it was met by a spectre, which proved either a hideous monster, or a guardian angel. It is to lead him across, or to scare him into the gulf. He asks his name, and is answered, "I am the spirit of thy life!"

To us nothing can appear more repugnant in itself, or more revolting to every feeling of reverence for the dead, than the exposure of the dead body; and our conclusion would be that the ancestral worship could not possibly have arisen amongst a people addicted to so horrid a practice. But the fact is, that their reverence followed the soul and not the flesh, and the corpse was disregarded by the survivors, having been abandoned by its own life. Porphyry has preserved to us a corresponding idea. He says, dead flesh is in itself not impure; but that of man is so, because having been united with a portion of the Divine spirit, when that departs it is rejected. Thus they fell upon the process which nature herself employs for preventing putrefaction. A Tartar brought to the capital of this kingdom, and made to comprehend the process of burial and its consequences, might, religious ideas apart, be as much filled with disgust and indignation as any traveller from Europe in witnessing the method practised in his country.

The Parsees have also, in this respect, alone, of the great systems, retained the original practice; and this is again important, as showing that the worship of the elements was, like Metempsychosis, a more recent invention. It is true, that they held burial, cremation, or the confiding of the ashes, or the body, to the waters, to be a sacrilege against the elements; but it does not follow that that was the motive which introduced, in the first instance, the exposure of the body to birds and beasts. The Chinese, as stated by Meng Tseou in the " earliest antiquity," threw out their parents into the ditches by the wayside; afterwards they hermetically closed them up in coffins, with the view of preventing the desecration of any of the elements :* the Hindus still specially set aside, at the funeral obsequies, a portion for dogs and ravens, as if in compensation for their vested right in the corpse.†

Turning to Tartary, we find conjointly practised all the methods of the Chinese, the Arians, the Buddhists, and the Hindus. They burn‡ the body, bury it, expose it to the air, immerse it in water, or abandon it to animals and birds.§ The last prevails amongst the tribes of the Desert.

"The true nomadic tribes," says Huc, "convey the dead to the tops of hills, or the bottoms of ravines, there to be devoured by the birds and beasts of prey. It is really horrible to travellers through the deserts of Tartary to see, as they constantly do, human remains, for which the eagles and wolves are contending."

In Thibet dogs are employed as sepulchres. The practice is so extraordinary in itself, and at the same time so valuable as a means of identifying races, in consequence of it having been

---

* "If the children allow no particle of earth to adhere to their bodies, what more can they desire?"—*Meng Tseou.*

† "The residue of the oblation to the gods must be left on a clean spot of ground as an oblation to all beings; intended, however, for dogs and crows in particular."—*As. Res.*, v. vii., p. 275.

‡ "The richer Tartars sometimes burn their dead with great solemnity. A large furnace of earth is constructed in a pyramidal form. Just before it is completed, the body is placed inside, standing, surrounded with combustibles. The edifice is then completely covered in, with the exception of a small hole at the bottom to admit fire, and another at the top, to give egress to the smoke, and keep up a current of air. During the combustion, the Lamas surround the tomb and recite prayers. The corpse being burnt they demolish the furnace, and remove the bones, which they carry to the grand Lama; he reduces them to a very fine powder, and having added to them an equal quantity of meal, he kneads the whole with care, and constructs with his own hands cakes of different sizes, which he places one upon the other, in the form of a pyramid."—*Huc.*

§ "At Chaprung, when any man of property dies, they take the body and bruise it to pieces, bones and all, and form it into balls, which they give to a very large sort of kites, who devour them. These birds are sacred, kept by the Lamas and fed by them, or by people appointed for the purpose, who alone approach them; others dare not go near them, perhaps from superstitious motives, for they are held in great fear."—*J. B. Fraser's Himalaya Mountains*, p. 338.

remarked by the ancients, that I collate a recent description of it in Thibet, with what has been reported of the ancient Parthians, Caspians, Hyrcanians, and Bactrians.

"This marvellous infinitude of dogs arises from the extreme respect which the Thibetians have for these animals, and the use to which they apply them in burying the dead. There are four different species of sepulture practised in Thibet; the first, combustion; the second, immersion in the rivers and lakes; the third, exposure on the summit of mountains; and the fourth, which is considered the most complimentary of all, consists in cutting the dead body in pieces, and giving these to be eaten by the dogs. The last method is by far the most popular. The poor have only as their mausoleum the common vagabond dogs of the locality; but the more distinguished defunct are treated with greater ceremony. In all the Lamaseries, a number of dogs are kept *ad hoc*, and within them the rich Thibetians are buried."

Justin says of the Parthians, that "their burial was effected by means of dogs and birds, and that the naked bones strewed the earth."

Porphyry relates the same of the Caspians.* Cicero says of the Hyrcanians, that the people supported *public dogs*—the chief men, private ones—each according to his faculty, to be torn by them; and that they deem this to be the best kind of sepulture.†
Of the Bactrians, Strabo says—" In the capital of Bactria they breed dogs, to *which they give a special name, which name, rendered into our language, means buriers.* The business of these dogs is to eat up all persons who are beginning to fall into decay, from old age or sickness. Hence it is that no tomb is visible in the suburbs of the town, while the town itself is all filled with human bones. It is said that Alexander abolished this custom."

The Turks have two names for dogs, independently of those of different breeds. The proper one is *Et* or *It;* but that in common use for those scavengers of the street is *Kopek;* kapak is to "cover." Though no longer used for the original purpose, they

---

* On Abstinence from Animal Food, b. iv., c. 21.
† Tusc. Questions, b. i., c. 45.

are maintained by the public for a similar one, and present the otherwise inexplicable anomaly of being at once objects of charity and aversion.

In the cuneiform inscription of Behistun, Darius no less than five times enumerates Sraddhas, but the translators, unacquainted with the ceremony, have not known what to make of the passages. Colonel Rawlinson has ingeniously made out the word which he renders *Thrada* to govern the sentence, and, after exhausting every etymological and constructive resource, translates it " performance " or " record," and supposes it to be some " allusion to the ancestors of Darius."* By the knowledge of this word, four or five other words connected with it might have been made out.

While borne on the full tide of discovery, and swept along by the breath of applause, the bark freighted with hieroglyphical investigation has well nigh been wrecked upon a sunken rock— the Chamber of Karnak. This is an apartment without windows, and only a single door, having all around in four rows the kings of Egypt arranged in a peculiar and anomalous fashion. They are placed back to back, beginning from a perpendicular line facing the entrance ; you see them as you enter, looking to the right and to the left, until at the extremities, on either side, there is the king whose name the chamber bears, Tothnes the 3rd, standing making his offering. But not only is he repeated on the right and on the left in face of these lines of Lares, but on each side he is figured twice in two compartments, one above the other. How so solemn a representation should have been enclosed in a secret chamber, shut out from the gaze of men, and yet not connected with a sepulchral edifice, remained a mystery wholly unfathomable. Nor less comprehensible, nor more reducible to any established order, was the number of these princes. The lists of Manetho and Eratosthanes were in vain sifted and assorted anew. The successions, as made out by previous inquiry, were re-examined afresh, but no key was found. The learned were at their wits'

---

* One of the passages in question he has thus translated :—" Former kings in succession (?) to them it is done as by me, by the grace of Ormud has been the performance of the whole (?) recorded."—*As. Soc.*, v. x., p. 250.

ends, but this was not all ; the names, as deciphered, were no less intractible than their numbers.*

Now, had any of the Egyptian travellers, who happened to be attended by a Hindu servant, thought of applying to him, and asking him to explain the enigma, he would have done so at once ; he would have told him, that it was *the Sraddha*, either *Kamya* or *Vridi;*† that is to say, a special Votive offering before undertaking a war, or upon its successful issue. If then asked if these ancestors were the predecessors of the king, he would have answered, " By no means ; they are his father, grandfather, great grandfather, great grandfather's brother, son, &c., on the paternal and maternal sides, and he presents them various offerings, making oblation with the part of his hand sacred to the manes." If asked, why they are placed back to back, and why the king does not perform the ceremony at once to all, he would answer, "They are so divided because they composed his paternal and maternal ancestors, the first of which are adored with their faces to the east, and the latter with their faces to the north."‡ If asked, why they were divided again into two sets, as the king is not repeated twice, but four times, he would answer, "There are two classes of progenitors ; the *Nandi-mukth*, or great ancestors, being addressed as *Pitris*, and as gods, are worshipped differently from *Viswadavas* or immediate ancestors ; and as there are four classes of ancestors, greater and lesser, paternal and maternal, so must there be four Sraddhas."§

Finally, if asked why so solemn a ceremony should be represented in a hidden and secret chamber, he would answer, "Because the ceremony itself could only be performed in a spot care-

---

* Bunsen, speaking of these discussions, says : " The English (Egyptologists) exhibit still grosser self-contradictions than the French and Italian critics."—*Egypt's Place*, &c., vol. i., p. 252.

† See Memoir of Mr. Colebrook in As. Res., v. vii.

‡ Vishnu Purana, book iii., chap. 15. It would be curious to know it the chamber is diagonally situated to the points of the compass.

§ He must severally dismiss, "First, the maternal ancestors, and then the gods ; and the order is the same with the maternal ancestors and the gods in respect to food, donation, and dismissal ; commencing with the washing of the feet until the dismissing of the Gods and Brahmins : the ceremonies are to be performed, first for paternal ancestors on the mother's side."— *Vishnu Purana*, p. 32.

fully enclosed; neither gods nor progenitors will partake of the food if the obsequial rite be looked at by a eunuch, an outcast, heretic, drunkard, sick or unclean person, mendicant, cock, or monkey."*

I cannot omit an identity in the form of adoration in the two ceremonies, and the form of expression in the two languages. "I adore with my arms" is the expression of the hieroglyphics. In the Puranas it is said, that a man having no means to perform the oblation shall repair to a forest and lift up his arms to the sun and other regions of the spheres, and say aloud, "I hope the progenitors will be satisfied with these arms tossed up in the air in devotion." When, then, Sir Gardiner Wilkinson treats the fact of the Indian sepoys, during the occupation of Egypt, prostrating themselves in the Egyptian temples as a mere result of their ignorance, and as an incident which might equally have happened in any Gothic cathedral which contained the sculpture of a cow, it is only to be regretted that he had not made himself better acquainted with the religion of Brahma, and the customs of Hindustan.

The connexion between the present and the future state was thereby established in such a manner as to interweave future punishments with present existence; assigning the terror of punishment inflicted in this world on those who had taken their departure for the next. This was the check imposed upon absolute power; this it was which secured the balance of the constitution without parliaments or press, and which gave a sanction to law beyond that of penal enactments; hence that maxim of Civism which Cicero lays down as constituting the highest excellence of a free state, according to which each man should consider his remotest ancestor, and his furthest posterity in the same light as his nearest living relative. This end was attained under those despotisms, from which the idea was transmitted, not by schools and philanthropy, but by *superstition.*

Amongst the Jews, of course, there was no ancestral sacrifice, but the traces of it as belonging to their old faith (that is to say, of the system to which Abraham had originally belonged) are impressed in indelible characters upon their ideas, laws, and in-

* Vishnu Purana, page 353. Consult also Colebrooke's Memoir on the "Ceremonies of the Hindus," "The Matsya Purana," "The Vayu."

stitutions.* To it we must refer the desire of children, the disgrace of a childless condition ; and if it were sought to interpret these feelings by general instincts, or considerations, the answer is to be found in the law by which the wife of the deceased brother, if he died childless, was taken by the next brother in order to raise up to him seed. The first child of such a marriage did not belong to the father but to the uncle, and inherited his property. This was the right of *Levirate*, which constitutes so important a chapter in their civil law. The case was one in which the property would not have gone out of the line, for there was the collateral male branch ; and the institutions of Moses, so particular in respect to the descent of property, did not regard the descent by the family, but by the tribe. The object was not to establish primogeniture. The institution was not based upon aristocratic power. Its purview was not class rights, but federal balance ; so that each of the twelve tribes of Judea should preserve its relative station in regard to the others, a provision justified by the event. The Levirate was therefore no portion of the system ; it was wholly extraneous, and is explicable only by the worship of the ancestors.

The lamentations of the Virgins of Israel over a premature death, is explained by us as losing the chance of giving birth to the Messiah ; but who explains in this fashion the parallel lament of the Grecian ?

It will not be denied, that the introduction of the injunction to honour father and mother into the Decalogue, and the placing of its neglect upon the same line as idolatry and murder, is fairly incomprehensible according to our notions either of faith or law ; but what are we to infer from the promise appended singly to that commandment, or, rather, the consequence which is to flow from its observance? "that thy days may be long in the land which the Lord, thy God, giveth thee." In what sense is this explained? If not explained, how is it accepted? Is it true that those who honour their parents are longlived, and those who do not honour them are shortlived ; and is it not in this sense that we repeat the words? The promise is not to the man, but to the

---

* "If thy father at all miss me then say, David earnestly asked leave of me that he might run to Bethlehem his city : for there is a yearly sacrifice (feast) there for all the family."—1 *Sam.* xx. 6.

people. The land which is given is the land of Judea, and the prolonged possession of it depended upon the observance of duty, and the possession of wisdom, which the ceremony of the Sraddha inculcated on its professsors, as the means by which the state itself was to be preserved; and this, in all times, was a truth neither strange nor unknown to a people who, though they had discarded the idolatry which had grown out of that antique and touching ceremony, had not forgotten the promptings of nature out of which it had arisen, nor dissevered political consequences from moral causes, the connexion of which it was calculated to enforce.

When first examining the monuments of Egypt, with a view of discovering any connexion with the East, and having fallen upon many points of minute and social resemblances, I was inclined to accept them as evidences of the derivation of the Hyksos from Tartary, attributing their introduction to the latter people; but after the ancestral faith broke upon me, it was with extreme surprise that I observed that, in the monuments of the old empire, prior to the Hyksos invasion, no gods whatever appear. In fact, the whole of the representations consist of Sraddhas, and the votive offerings are precisely those of the Institutes of Menu and of the early Hindoos, which afford the explanation wanting in Egypt. Sir Gardiner Wilkinson bears upon this point the following conclusive testimony :—

"The only appearance of a man having the character of a deity, occurs in the temple built by Thothmes III. at Samneh, where Osirtasen III. is represented performing the same offices as a god; but we do not know how far he was assimilated to a deity, and he merely wears a *royal* cap. There are also offerings of kings, as of other persons, to their deceased parents; but these are only made to them in the character they assumed after death, when they received the name of Osiris, from being supposed to return, after a virtuous life, to the great origin from which they were emanations. Sometimes the king even offers to a figure of himself and his queen, seated on thrones, before whom he stands as an officiating priest."

In the return of the soul to its source, we have the *ferver* of the Arians, and indeed the name of Osiris occurs in the Vendidat as *gah*, or regent of the declining sun. The oblation of the

Sraddha to the living as well as to the dead, was not unknown
to the Hindus. In their ritual this passage occurs :—

" May those in my family, who have been burnt by fire, or
who are alive and yet unburnt, be satisfied with this food presented on the ground, and proceed contented towards the supreme
path (of eternal bliss)."—*As. Res.*, v. vii., p. 252.

We thus see the progress of faith running parallel in Hindustan and in Egypt ; the ancestors worshipped as gods, and the
gods reigning as kings, for the gods of the old world, that is,
of the idolatrous one, were the lares of sovereigns. These
Pantheistic associations point not only to a common faith, but to
an original race. After those personages, with whom we are
acquainted, or at least with whose names we are familiar, had
passed to the rank of Divinities, belief might be propagated by the
ordinary methods of conversion ; but in the original form that
was impracticable ; not only initiation but affiliation was required.
The religion of the forefathers so reached in the first instance
Egypt, Phœnicia, Greece, and Italy, as seen in the Heroes,
Manes, Lares, Patres, and Penates, constituting at once a
general faith and genealogical bond in particular families.
So the distinction of the deities of the " Majorum et Minorum
Gentium," reproduces the greater and lesser Ancestors of the
Sraddha. This supposes not merely instructors in the primitive
faith, but rulers of the original race ; nor was it that race which
disseminated and multiplied itself, for then the varieties of speech
would be inexplicable. As Cecrops and Cadmus, as Pelasgus
and Inachus, were strangers, who came to the West bringing
with them rites and letters ; so, although removed in date, must
Menes be held a " Manu " from the Himalaya.

Whatever theoretical or social distinctions may have arisen in
the religion of Asia, they noways interfered with the uniformity
of this ceremonial, which was in rites identical from the Yellow
Sea to the Mediterranean, and to Abyssinia. The objects
figured on the monuments of that Egypt, which 2000 years ago
descended to the tomb, correspond with the Chinese oblations
2500 years before that period, and with those offered to this hour
in Hindustan. The eldest of religious practices remains as firmly
seated to-day as the oldest of human monuments ; and as the
pyramids stand amongst structures, so amongst ceremonies does
the Sraddha.

We arrive at a most startling conclusion : that from a tribe whom we have been accustomed to consider, if warlike, savage—and if conquering, stupid—has proceeded the whole mass of the metaphysical ideas and religious sentiment, no less than the arts of the ancient world.*

* The Tablets representing the ancestors, or the carving into their likeness of the case which contained the body, must have been the first employment for the sculptor's chisel and the painter's brush.

NOTE.

HINDOO LAW OF ADOPTION.

Menu's Institute.

By the eldest, at the moment of his birth, the father, having begotten a son, discharges his debt to his own progenitors.

That son alone, by whom he discharges his debt, and through whom he attains immortality, was begotten from a sense of duty; all the rest are considered by the wise as begotten from love of pleasure.

By a son, a man obtains victory over all people; by a son's son, he enjoys immortality; and afterwards, by a son of that grandson, he reaches the solar abode.

Since the son (tráyaté) delivers his father from the hell named *put*, he was therefore called puttra by Brahma himself.

A son given must never claim the family and estate of his natural father; the funeral cake follows the family and estate; but of him who has *given away his son* the funeral oblation is extinct.

A son of any description must be anxiously adopted by one who has none: for the sake of the funeral cake, water, and solemn rites; and for the celebrity of his name.

Daya-Crama Sangraha.

But a grandson whose father is dead, and a great grandson, whose father and grandfather are dead, participate equally in the inheritance with the son, for they, without distinction, confer equal benefits on the deceased owner of the property, by the presentation to him of funeral offerings at solemn obsequies.

Gentoo Laws.

If a man has neither son, grandson, nor grandson's son, all his property goes to his adopted son; if there be no adopted son, it goes to the adopted son's son; if there be no adopted son's son, it goes to the adopted son's grandson.

If there be no adopted son's grandson, then, if the property has already been divided among the heirs, it goes to the wife; if it has not been divided, it goes to the brother; but the wife shall receive food and clothes.

He who is desirous to adopt a child must inform the magistrates thereof, and shall perform the jugg, and shall give gold and rice to the father of the child whom he would adopt; then, supposing the child not to have had his ears bored, or to have received the Brahminical thread, or to have been married in his father's house, and not to be five years old, if the father will give up such a child, or if the mother gives him up by order of the father, and there are other brothers of that child, such a child shall be adopted.

MACNAGHTEN'S HINDOO LAW,

I have proceeded far enough to be satisfied of my own incompetency to the work which I have undertaken ; and from what I have already said upon the subject of adoption, the difficulty of laying down rules concerning it *cannot but have been sufficiently apparent.*

In the case of Veerapermal Pillay *v.* Narain Pillay, the Recorder of Madras says, "The general rule of the Hindoo law certainly is, that an only or eldest son ought not to be given in adoption ; because he has the obsequies of his natural ancestors to attend to ; and adoption as completely transfers him from his own family as though he had never belonged to it."

In omitting to adopt a son, an offence even is incurred. On defect of any son in general, exclusion from heaven is declared in the text, "*Heaven awaits not one destitute of a son.*"

Nothing in the Hindoo law is more peremptorily interdicted than the gift of an only son in adoption ; even the gift of an eldest son is forbidden as sinful.

In the Brahman, Khettry, and Boice castes, a child whom it would have been incest to beget cannot be adopted. The son of a sister or of a daughter, therefore, cannot be adopted by a Brahman, Khettry, or Boice.

I have been favoured by a translation from the Sanscrit on the subject of adoption. This work, I am sorry to say, is still in manuscript. It is more concise and *less unintelligible* than any Hindoo tract that has fallen into my hands.

The sum of all I have been able to collect out of books or from living authorities is, that in the three superior classes, if there be brothers of the whole blood, a son of one of them will for religious purposes be the son of all ; and that while this son exists, the childless brothers by the same father and mother, need not adopt one for the performance of sacred rites. But that in a secular point of view a male child is not considered as the son of his father's brethren, and that to take the heritage as a son of his uncle he must be adopted ; that, spiritually considered, he confers benefits as a son upon his uncles ; that, temporally considered, he does not as a son derive any benefits from them—and that the son of a brother is recommended in preference to all others for adoption.